N 450

Grandparents Around the World

DORKA RAYNOR

ALBERT WHITMAN & Company, Chicago

"Those we loved
gave form and substance to our beings . . .
Love binds the generations one to another."

In memory of my "Babcia,"
the grandmother who enchanted my childhood,
and for Sevek and John,
and Lilah and Jesse

Library of Congress Cataloging in Publication Data

Raynor, Dorka.
  Grandparents around the world.

  SUMMARY: Presents forty-six full page photographs of grandparents and children taken in
twenty-five countries with a brief identifying
text accompanying each photograph.
  1. Grandparents—Pictorial works—Juvenile
literature. [1. Grandparents—Pictorial works]
I. Title.
HQ759.9.R39   301.42'7   76-57661
ISBN 0-8075-3037-9

1 Out for
a walk,
Île de Ré,
France

Geweiht dem
Denken an Joh:Jos:
Imseng 1806-1869
Kilchherr von Saas
und Bergfuehrer
Erschliesser der von
Gott erschaffenen
Schoenheiten der
Saaser Bergwelt
Gestiftet von Jakob
...er Langenthal

TISSOT

3   Luxembourg Gardens, Paris, France

2   After church, Saas-Fée, Switzerland

4   After baptism, Lebanese family, Casablanca, Morocco

5   Châteaudun, France

6
Gypsies
in Lisbon,
Portugal

7   Bali, Indonesia

8   An English grandfather

9 Swimming lesson, Germany

11   In Brittainy, France

10   Crete, Greece

12   Marrakech, Morocco

14 Morocco

15 Nepal

16-17 The widows,
Vitoria, Spain

18 To market, Isfahan, Iran

19 Off to the hayfield, Switzerland

20 An excursion, Taiwan

21 At Otavalo market, Ecuador

22 Three generations, Hong Kong

24   Waiting for the bus, Fez, Morocco

25   Sicilian wedding guests, Italy

26 Tokyo, Japan

29 Serres, France

30 Oaxaca, Mexico

31   Old Jerusalem, Israel

34 After the wedding, Italy

Parade watchers, Tunis, Tunisia

36　The Bahamas

37 Jordanian shop

39   After school, Soria, Spain

40 South of France

42   Palamós, Costa Brava, Spain

44   Fez, Morocco

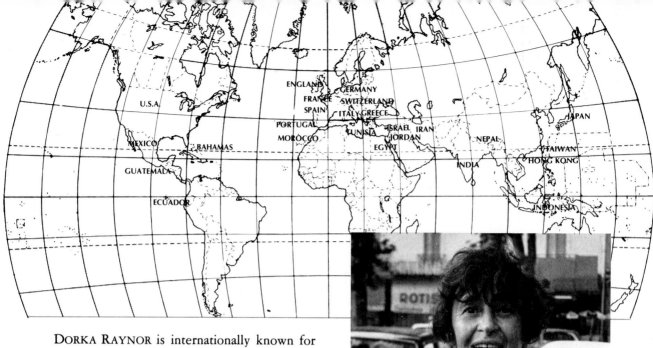

DORKA RAYNOR is internationally known for her photographs of children. Her prints in permanent museum collections include those on pages 16-17, in the Metropolitan Museum of Art, New York City, and on page 40, in the Art Institute of Chicago. Mrs. Raynor, whose home is in Winnetka, Illinois, has been honored by the American Society of Magazine Photographers and awarded prizes in France. Her photographs have been published in Switzerland and Japan and used extensively in textbooks in the United States. Her own published collection, *This Is My Father and Me* (Albert Whitman), is a loving tribute to the place fathers hold in their children's hearts.

A. Hyatt Mayor, author of *Popular Prints of the Americas* (Crown) and *Prints and People, a Social History of Printed Pictures* (Metropolitan Museum and New York Graphics Society), wrote of Mrs. Raynor's special talent, "You are a force of joy in this age of apprehension. The world just cannot be heading for quite such a catastrophe when you find the same tenderness, the same exquisite communion in all costumes and all lands. You will bring happiness to thousands by sensitively recording the happiness of a few dozen."

COUNTRIES PICTURED

Bahamas, 36
Ecuador, 21
Egypt, 27
England, 8
France, 1, 3, 5, 11, 29, 40, 43
Germany, 9

Greece, 10
Guatemala, 33
Hong Kong, 22, 32
India, 28
Indonesia, 7
Iran, 18
Israel, 31

Italy, 25, 34, 45
Japan, title page, 13, 26
Jordan, 37
Mexico, 30
Morocco, 4, 12, 14, 24, 44
Nepal, 15

Portugal, 6, 41
Spain, 16-17, 38, 39, 42; cover
Switzerland, 2, 19
Taiwan, 20
Tunisia, 35
United States, 23